QUIN MCMEN'S ZOMBIE DISCOVERY

BY LEAH COFFEY

AuthorHouse™
1663 Liberty Drive
Bloomington, IN 47403
www.authorhouse.com
Phone: 1 (800) 839-8640

Published by AuthorHouse 08/21/2019

ISBN: 978-1-5462-6884-0 (sc)
ISBN: 978-1-5462-6883-3 (e)

Library of Congress Control Number: 2018913632

Print information available on the last page.

This book is printed on acid-free paper.

author HOUSE®

QUIN MCMEN'S ZOMBIE DISCOVERY

LEAH COFFEY

Have you ever heard of a zombie?
Of course you have, how silly of me.

They are easy to picture, just close your eyes
and you will see.

I have always envisioned them with blood
shot eyes and toxic green skin,
covered in bubbly boils that come from within.

They are said to be the living dead
and eat brains to stay fed.

They wear torn clothes as if they had been mauled by a bear,
but I think it was the worms when they
were buried, you know where.

Let us of course not forget a few missing
finger tips or maybe some toes
or even a nose!

All you hear are moans when they walk;
I guess that should not be such a shock.

After all they are missing plenty of teeth
and oh goodness grief their breath really reeks!

My name is Quin, Quin McMen if you please.
I am one of the only ones left that can
still sit and feel the breeze.

Has everyone's brains turned to mush?
I must admit I miss my friends so very much!

I always thought zombies were easy to spot,
but here is the lesson I was taught.

It is a plague I say! A disease you see,
that you will not get from a sneeze.

Being plugged in
is supposedly how you win,
but do not be fooled
or you might turn into a ghoul.

With blood shot eyes glued to those screens,
they are buried down deep
at least six feet!

Their flesh is the same
with blood pumping veins
that gives warmth to a body
that eats chicken teriyaki!

With clothes so pristine
or so it may seem.

A jacket is left on a bench and a shoe lace is left untied.
My guess is someone is going to take a tumbling ride!

I have seen them stumbling around
following the crowd going round, round, round.

15

They say not a word
when they are gathered in a herd.

All eyes are glazed
as if they are locked in a haze,
looking down into a bleak static maze.

I ask myself have they gone so astray?
Will they ever come back or is it a trip one way?

Do I have to mention
to pay attention!
Watch out for that tree
or better yet watch out for me!

I dip, dive and dodge my way around,
all the way through this little town.

17

I prefer living life, looking up to the clouds
with my feet firmly planted on the ground.

And no, I do not mean the cyber cloud
where you store your life until you feel endowed.

I'd rather roll the dice
and not think twice.

I want to hear someone's laughter
and find my happily ever after.

How did anyone get the notion
that I wanted to read emotion?

I rather feel happy or even sad;
I mean I am not wishing to be a nomad.

But let us get a grip
and not follow what is supposed to be hip.

Instead let us stand in awe
of this world we live in with friends, family, teachers and all!

Printed in the United States
By Bookmasters